FRANKIE'S
MAGIC
FOOTBALL

BY FRANK LAMPARD

Frankie vs The Pirate Pillagers

Frankie vs The Rowdy Romans

Frankie vs The Cowboy's Crew

Frankie vs The Mummy's Menace

Frankie vs The Knight's Nasties

Frankie and the World Cup Carnival

Frankie and the Dragon Curse

FRANKIE AND THE
WORLD CUP CARNIVAL

FRANK LAMPARD

LITTLE, BROWN BOOKS FOR YOUNG READERS
www.lbkids.co.uk

LITTLE, BROWN BOOKS FOR YOUNG READERS

First published in Great Britain in 2014 by
Little, Brown Books for Young Readers
Reprinted 2014 (twice)

Copyright © 2014 by Lamps On Productions

The moral right of the author has been asserted.

A CIP catalogue record for this book
is available from the British Library.

978-0-349-12443-8

Typeset in Cantarell by M Rules
Printed and bound in Great Britain by
Clays Ltd, St Ives plc

Papers used by LBYR are from well-managed forests
and other responsible sources.

MIX
Paper from
responsible sources
FSC
www.fsc.org FSC® C104740

Little, Brown Books for Young Readers
An imprint of
Little, Brown Book Group
100 Victoria Embankment
London EC4Y 0DY

An Hachette UK Company
www.hachette.co.uk

www.lbkids.co.uk

To my mum Pat, who encouraged me to do my homework in between kicking a ball all around the house, and is still with me every step of the way.

Welcome to a fantastic
Fantasy League — the greatest
football competition ever held
in this world or any other!

You'll need four on a team,
so choose carefully. This is a lot
more serious than a game in the
park. You'll never know who your
next opponents will be, or
where you'll face them.

So lace up your boots, players,
and good luck! The whistle's
about to blow!

The Ref

PART ONE

CHAPTER 1

"Budge up!" said Louise, as she came into the living room, carrying a bowl of crisps. Frankie shifted along the couch, pressing right up against Charlie.

"I can't go any further," grumbled Charlie, pointing with his goalie gloves to Max, Frankie's pet dog.

He was curled up at the end of the sofa, asleep. "I thought dogs slept in baskets, anyway."

Max opened one eye and growled softly.

"Not *that* dog," said Frankie, laughing. "He just wants to watch the game with the rest of us."

"He's asleep!" said Charlie.

It was half-time in the World Cup semi-final, and England were one-all with Argentina. At stake was a place in the Final against Brazil, where the tournament was taking place. Frankie had to pinch himself – no one had thought England would get this far. Especially not his dad. He'd booked a table at a posh restaurant for himself and Frankie's mum on the night of the semi-final. He'd never thought this meant he might actually miss an England game!

Which meant there was more room on the sofa for Frankie and his friends.

Charlie was trying to get a crisp from the bowl, but he was struggling to pick one up.

"Why not take your gloves off?" said Frankie, knowing what the answer would be.

"No can do," said Charlie. "A goalkeeper's always got to be ready."

Frankie and Louise shared a

smile. Sometimes Charlie took things too far.

The TV was showing a replay of the other semi-final between Brazil and Germany. The game had been won when Ricardo, the nineteen-year-old Brazilian striker, had scored an incredible overhead kick in the last minute of the game. The fans were already calling it a "Ricardo". The TV showed the kick from several angles, normal speed and in slow-motion. Frankie could only shake his head in amazement. The commentator was talking about how Ricardo had grown up very poor in a slum, living in a single room with his four sisters.

"I wish I could score a goal like that," said Frankie.

"I bet you could," said Louise.

Frankie shrugged. It was all very well scoring a great goal, but to do it in a game as important as a semi-final was another thing entirely.

"Imagine the pressure he was under!" said Charlie.

Frankie heard footsteps pounding down the stairs and his brother Kevin burst into the room wearing a pristine Brazil kit. The only downside to his parents being out was that Kevin had to stay in to babysit.

"What's the score, babies?" he said.

He shoved Max on to the floor, then flopped on to the sofa. Louise's bowl of crisps spilt all over Charlie. Max grabbed a few from the carpet, then scampered back to his basket.

"It's one–all," said Frankie, trying not to get irritated. *Kevin's not much of a fan if he hasn't even watched the first half,* he thought.

Kevin snatched the remaining crisps from Louise's lap and stuffed a handful into his mouth. "I bet England lose," he said. "They always lose."

Louise glared at him. "Come on, Frankie," she said. "Let's go out into the garden and have a kickabout.

There's still five minutes until the second half starts."

Charlie followed Louise through the French doors and into the garden, but first Frankie went to the back of the kitchen. In the cupboard under the sink were two balls. One was a few weeks old, and the other was a battered peeling wreck that barely bounced. Only a few people knew its secret. He grinned to himself, recalling all the adventures they'd had, thanks to his magic football. Well, tonight he didn't want an adventure – he just wanted a quick game with his friends, then back to the second half. He took the good ball and closed the cupboard door.

It was a warm evening with clear blue skies. The neighbourhood was quiet, with everyone indoors watching the game. Frankie bounced the ball a couple of times on his foot, then kicked it to Louise. She controlled it under her trainer.

"Why not try that kick, Frankie?" she said. "I'll kick it up for you."

Frankie smiled. "Okay. You ready, Charlie?"

His friend had taken up position by the fence. The gap between two fence-posts was the goal they normally used.

"Always ready," said Charlie, spreading his gloves.

Louise chipped the ball into the air, and Frankie watched it sail towards him over his shoulder. At the last moment, he flicked his body backwards.

"Loser!" shouted a voice.

Frankie's foot skimmed the ball and he landed in a heap on his back.

"Are you all right, Frankie?" asked Louise, rushing over.

Frankie rubbed his back, sitting up gingerly. His brother Kevin was at the back door, doubled over laughing.

"He put me off," said Frankie.

Kevin straightened up. "Always making excuses," he said. He disappeared for a moment, then returned carrying the magic football. "Hey, you might have more luck with this one instead."

"Just be careful with it," said Frankie. He wished his brother had never found out about the ball's secret, but it was too late now.

"Why?" said Kevin, dribbling the ball into the garden. "Scared?"

"Of course not," said Frankie.

"Hey, freckle-face," shouted Kevin. "Save this."

He blasted the ball at Charlie, who caught the ball easily.

"Great save, Charlie," said Louise.

Kevin blushed. "Give me another go. I was just practising with that one."

Frankie ran and retrieved the magic ball from beside the fence. He held it close to his chest. "That's enough," he said. "We shouldn't mess around with the ball. You know what it can do."

Kevin's shoulders sagged. "All right," he said. "You win."

He lunged forward suddenly and knocked the ball from Frankie's hands, then turned and kicked it hard. The fence shook as the ball bounced off it.

"Why not play with the other ball?" said Charlie.

"I prefer this one," said Kevin. He swung his foot again.

Frankie couldn't do anything as the ball flew through the French doors and into the lounge.

CRASH!

CHAPTER 2

Kevin's face went white and he stared after the football.

Frankie glanced at his friends, hardly daring to go in and see what was broken.

A second later, Max trotted to the doorstep, tail between his legs.

Frankie approached the French

doors slowly, and saw the TV lying on its side in the living room, with glass strewn across the carpet. He couldn't see the ball anywhere.

"Oh no!" said Louise.

"Nice one," said Charlie.

"It . . . it wasn't my fault," said Kevin.

Frankie felt dread building in the bottom of his stomach. His parents would be fuming. They were always telling him not to play football indoors.

"We'd better clear up the mess," he said quietly.

There were no more smart comments from Kevin as they swept

up the glass and set the TV upright again. Frankie couldn't help glancing at the clock on the wall. Two hours until his parents got back. More importantly, it was one minute until the second half began and now they had no TV to watch it on.

"We can go to mine if you want," said Charlie. "My mum will be watching her dancing programme, but we've got a spare TV in the garage."

"Thanks," said Louise.

"What about me?" asked Kevin.

Charlie looked long and hard at Frankie's brother, and Frankie expected him to say "no".

"All right," said Charlie. "Just promise not to break anything."

As Frankie was locking the back door, he couldn't help glancing at the TV. Perhaps he should call his mum now on her mobile, just to let her know. He went to the phone hanging on the wall and dialled her number.

She picked up on the third ring. "What's wrong?" she said straight away. "Has Max swallowed another golf ball?"

"No, Mum," said Frankie. "Max is fine."

In fact, Max was sniffing around the bottom of the TV, whining oddly.

"So what's the matter?" said his mum. "We've only just had our starters."

"There's been a little . . ." Frankie paused. Was it his imagination, or were there lights sparkling around the TV? "... accident," he finished.

Max was backing away, heckles up.

"Accident?" said his mother, her voice shrill. "Is someone hurt? Where's Kevin?"

A picture was swimming in and out of focus on the remains of the cracked screen.

Frankie moved closer with the phone still clutched to his ear.

"Frankie?" said his mother. "Are you still there?"

More sparks, like tiny stars, were hovering in front of the TV. It wasn't an electrical fault, Frankie knew that much.

"It's Frankie," his mother was saying to his dad. "I don't know . . . an accident, he said . . ."

A face appeared on the screen – one that Frankie would have recognised anywhere.

"Ricardo!" he gasped.

"Pardon, but what is 'Ricardo'?" said his mother.

"Nothing, Mum," said Frankie. "Got to go."

He hung up the phone and approached the TV slowly. The Brazilian superstar was peering out. "Hello?" he said.

Is he talking to me? Frankie wondered.

By now, Charlie, Louise and Kevin had come back into the room. "What's going on?" asked Louise. She did a double-take at the TV. "Oh, it's working again."

"Is anyone there?" said Ricardo.

"We're here," said Frankie.

"This isn't possible," said Kevin. "The TV is *not* talking to us."

"*I'm* talking to you," said Ricardo. He held up the magic football.

"I assume this belongs to one of you?"

"It's mine," said Frankie, holding up his hand.

Ricardo nodded, and pointed right at Frankie's face. "Right, have you got a team?"

Frankie looked at his friend. "Yes, but . . ."

"Come on, then," said the Brazilian. "I need your help."

"Come on where?" said Charlie.

"There isn't time to explain," said Ricardo. "The World Cup is at stake."

The hairs on Frankie's arms prickled. "How do we get to you?"

Ricardo shrugged. "How should I know? It's *your* ball!"

Max began rooting round on the sofa, getting his nose down the side of the cushion.

"Now isn't the time to be hunting for crisps," said Charlie.

But when Max withdrew his nose, he was clutching the remote

control. It was sparkling too. Frankie took it off him, and pointed it at the TV. "Here goes nothing," he said, and pressed the "On" button.

A sudden wind whipped through the room, tugging at his clothes. He heard a shriek and turned to see Louise with her hair lashing her face. Crisps blew up around them, and Max's paws scrabbled on the carpet. Frankie realised he was being pulled towards the TV, and grabbed the edge of the sofa.

Kevin struggled across the floor, leaning into the wind. Charlie had latched his gloves around the door-frame.

With a bark, Max was lifted from the carpet and flew into the TV, vanishing in a silver flash.

Next Kevin shot past, arms flailing. He barrelled into Louise and they both tumbled through the TV and disappeared. Only Frankie and Charlie remained.

"Don't fight it!" said Frankie, over the roaring rush of the gale. "Let go after three! One . . . two . . ."

Charlie hurtled past with a wail.

"Three!" Frankie said to himself. He let go of the couch and let the hurricane take him.

CHAPTER 3

The world went dark for a few seconds, then Frankie realised he could hear distant chanting. He could smell sweat and grass and leather.

He opened his eyes and found himself in a changing room, with shirts hanging on pegs, and other kit strewn on benches. His friends were all around him, their faces puzzled. Max gave himself a shake.

"Nice of you to join me," said a voice.

They all span round and saw Ricardo standing behind them wearing a tracksuit and holding the magic football. Frankie couldn't believe he was there in the flesh.

"Hi," was all he managed to say.

Ricardo looked Frankie up and down, then glanced at the others. "You look very young to have the football," he said.

"I won it at a fair," said Frankie, feeling a bit stupid.

"We've won every game we've played so far," said Louise, lifting her chin proudly.

"Best goal-keeping record in the fantasy league," added Charlie.

Max wagged his tail. "Toughest defence on four legs too," he barked.

Frankie grinned — it was nice to have a *talking* dog again.

Kevin, for once, didn't say anything at all. He hadn't been a part of their team, until today.

"Well, this challenge will be a lot tougher than anything you've faced before," said the Brazilian.

Frankie stepped forward. "We're ready. You said the World Cup was in trouble?"

Ricardo sagged on to a bench, placing the ball beside him. He nodded gravely. "Three items have been stolen," he said. "Without them, the Final will not happen."

"What are they?" asked Charlie.

Ricardo counted them off on his fingers. "The head referee's whistle, the ball that will kick-off the Final and, last of all, the trophy itself."

"Can't you call the police?" asked Kevin.

The Brazilian laughed emptily. "The police can't help with this," he said. "A magical problem requires a magical solution."

"So can't they just find another ball and another whistle?" said Kevin.

Ricardo shook his head. "You don't understand. These objects aren't just *things.* They have magical properties. The ball gives the players skills, the whistle ensures fair play, and the trophy — that's the most important of the three — is the spirit of football itself, the object which drives teams to win."

Kevin scoffed. "I don't believe it," he said.

Frankie glared at his brother, but Ricardo simply walked to the door. "Follow me, and I'll show you," he said.

As soon as he opened the door, Frankie heard the noise of the roaring crowd. "We're in a stadium, aren't we?"

Ricardo led them down a tunnel, and the noise grew louder all the time. At the end, he pointed. "Not just any stadium."

Frankie rocked back on his heels as he saw the white shirts of the players on the pitch and the huge stands on every side. "It's England and Argentina," he said. "We're in Brazil!"

The others huddled around him as they watched the second half of the game. The score, so the display said, was still one-all. But something was wrong. One player missed the ball completely and slid over. Another tripped over his own feet.

"The changes are happening already," said Ricardo. "They are losing their skills, you see?"

Two Argentine players jumped for the same ball and banged heads. They lay on the ground, groaning. Then an England defender slid in for a tackle – on the referee! The crowd started to boo and hiss.

"Okay, even I believe you," said Kevin. "What can we do?"

As Ricardo took them back to the tunnel, Frankie felt despair growing in the pit of his stomach. *Four years of waiting for the World Cup are going to end in catastrophe unless I can do something about it.*

But this sounded far tougher than the other challenges they'd faced.

In the dressing room again, Ricardo pulled out a boot bag from beneath a bench, and opened it carefully. Inside were a pair of boots, gold in colour. Frankie recognised them at once as Ricardo's. "These will take you where you need to go," he said. He handed them to Frankie.

Frankie turned the boots over in his hands. "But they won't fit."

"Try them on," said the Brazilian with a faint smile.

Frankie pulled on the boots, which were at least five sizes too big. "Told you," he said, as he laced them up.

"You'd better take this too," said Ricardo, throwing the ball to Frankie.

As soon as he caught it, he felt the boots tighten on his feet. They shrank in front of his eyes until they fit perfectly.

"Wow!" said Frankie.

"Hang on," said Charlie. "Why don't you recover the missing items?"

The Brazilian checked his watch. "Because," he said, "I'm due at a press conference in five minutes, then I've got physio. I can't just vanish into thin air. The magic football brought you guys here for a reason. It's up to you now."

Frankie's feet began to tingle. "Something's happening!" he said.

Ricardo took a step back. "Good luck, team," he said, and waved.

"Wait!" said Louise. "You never told us *who* stole the items."

Before Ricardo could answer, the dressing room vanished.

CHAPTER 4

Frankie found himself surrounded by looming trees. A canopy of branches above them blocked out most of the sun, but it was so hot sweat prickled over his skin. Vines hung from the trees, wrapping themselves round the trunks. All around were colourful plants and huge ferns.

"This can't be right," he said. "Why are we in the jungle?"

"Maybe the boots are broken," said Charlie, batting away a fly with his glove.

"It's the rainforest," said Louise. "The river Amazon flows through Brazil, remember?"

"Great!" said Kevin. "How are we supposed to get home?"

Max's ears pricked up. "Did you hear that?"

Louise shook his head. "Hear what?"

Frankie hadn't heard anything either.

"*That*!" said Max. "I can't help it if dogs have more sensitive hearing than humans."

Then Frankie heard something too. A distant, shrill sound. "A whistle!" he said.

"It's weird, aren't jungles supposed to be noisy?" said Charlie. "Where are all the animals?"

He was right. The rainforest was silent. The only sound Frankie could hear was their own feet in the undergrowth.

And the whistle.

"It's coming from over there," he said to the others, pointing between the trees.

Max went first, nose to the ground. They climbed over the huge gnarled roots of the trees, and all the time the whistle grew louder. Frankie peered around. He couldn't help feeling they were being watched. The forest was so dark he could only see a few metres ahead. Was that a shadow passing between the trees? He strained his eyes, but couldn't make anything out.

Eventually they reached a small clearing. The few branches overhead were loaded with green and orange mangoes. They were halfway across the clearing when Max stopped dead.

"What is it?" said Frankie.

A low growl sounded from the trees. "Uh-oh," said Charlie.

A set of yellow eyes peered from the gloom. Then another. "Double uh-oh," said Louise.

Pairs of eyes appeared all around them, then one by one, six or seven big black cats prowled into the clearing. Jaguars. Their teeth were as long as Frankie's fingers.

Charlie had picked up a stick from the ground.

"Ooh, now I'm scared," said one of the jaguars, chuckling.

Frankie stood in front of his friends. "We don't mean you any harm," he said. "We're just here to find a whistle."

"Is that right?" said the jaguar. "Well, we have orders to eat anyone who's trying to find the whistle."

"You and your big mouth," muttered Kevin, shrinking even further back.

Max puffed out his chest and stood as tall as he could – which was about up to Frankie's knees. "Orders from who?"

"Never you mind," said jaguar. "Any last requests?"

Frankie threw the ball up and kicked it as high as he could into the sky. It smacked into one of the branches, and hundreds of mangoes fell to the ground.

Thump! Thump–thump–thump!

The jaguars dodged this way and that as the fruits smacked down.

"Run!" said Frankie.

They sprinted away from the big cats, plunging back into the forest. Frankie didn't even bother to look back – he knew the mango downpour wouldn't keep their enemies busy for long.

At last, panting for breath, they stopped behind a huge trunk.

"I think we lost them," said Louise. "Quick thinking, Captain!"

"But I also lost my magic football," said Frankie.

"No, you didn't," said Charlie. He held up the football in his gloves. "I caught it!"

Kevin emerged from the undergrowth last. He had mango stains down his shirt. "This will never come out!" he said.

"Better than being lunch, though," said a voice above them.

They all looked up to see a monkey sitting on a branch. "Hi," said Frankie.

"You should hide," he said, casting nervous glances about. "Before Ali sees you."

The whistle went again, and the monkey jumped to another branch. "Gotta go."

"Hey, wait!" said Frankie. But the hairy creature was gone.

More confused than ever, Frankie and his friends walked along the riverbank in the same direction as the monkey. *Who's Ali?* Frankie wondered. *Is he the one who stole the objects?*

Soon they came to a place where the trees met the river, and one of the strangest sights Frankie had ever seen. Several alligators were lounging in the shallows, and beside each one sat a monkey holding a huge fern branch and using it as a fan. Parrots were waiting by and whenever a crocodile opened its mouth, one would peck at the dirty teeth. Some of the crocodiles were on their backs, while monkeys itched their bellies with sticks.

"I've not seen a lot of wildlife programmes," said Max, "but this doesn't look entirely natural."

The alligators stirred together,

shifting their bulky bodies to make a channel between them. Frankie saw why — a huge alligator was heading towards them, gliding on the water. Weirdly, it wasn't using its tail to swim — it was being dragged by two snakes, their heads just above the water.

"That's seriously lazy," muttered Charlie.

Frankie felt a jolt of surprise as he saw that the massive alligator was wearing a cord over its ridged snout. "The whistle!" he whispered to his friends, pointing.

"How can we get it?" asked Charlie.

"Are those gloves bite-proof?" asked Kevin.

"Very funny," said Charlie.

"Maybe we can just reason with it," said Louise.

A low chuckle made them all spin around. The jaguars were back, covered in sticky pulp and looking unhappy. "Yes, you try reasoning with Ali," said the leader of the cats. "Now, move it!"

Frankie and his friends let the jaguars escort them to the shoreline of the river. The alligators turned one by one and watched them with cold stares. The one with the whistle was enjoying a back-rub from two monkeys. *He must be Ali,* Frankie thought. *It's like he's got the whole jungle doing what he wants.*

"We found these intruders," said the jaguar. "They're looking for the whistle."

Ali bared his teeth in what might have been a smile. "Is that right?" he said.

"It was stolen," said Frankie, aware of all the teeth close by. "We've come to get it back."

"Well, in that case, I should just give it you," said Ali.

"Really?" said Kevin.

"Er . . . not quite," said the alligator. "There's one condition –

you have to pass a test. A football trial to be precise."

"Do crocodiles play football?" asked Max.

"Oh, how many times!" said Ali, "I AM NOT A CROCODILE. Of course crocodiles don't play football!"

"Sorry," said Max. "It's just you look like a croco . . ."

Ali snapped his jaws. "So will you accept the challenge?"

"Yes," said Frankie, without hesitation.

Kevin grabbed his arm. "Wait!" he whispered. "Don't you think you should find out what the challenge is first?"

"We don't have a choice," said
Frankie. "You saw the England
game. Someone could get injured if
we don't get the whistle back and
restore fair play."

"Right," said Ali. "Your job is
simple. One of your team has to
kick the football across the river —
from one bank to the other."

Frankie's heart sank as he gazed
across the huge river.

"It's too far," said Charlie. "It's
impossible."

"Not my problem," said the
alligator. He was definitely smiling
now. It was a very toothy grin.

CHAPTER 5

Frankie looked at his friends. *What have I agreed to?* he thought. *Charlie's right — the river is too wide. Even the England goalkeeper couldn't hoof it that far!*

"You can have three goes," said Ali, "since I'm feeling generous."

"Let me try," said Kevin, grabbing

the ball from Charlie. "I've got the hardest kick."

He placed the ball on the ground, took a few steps back, then blasted it high. Frankie watched the ball sail across the water, then the wind caught it and it plopped into the river about halfway across.

"Rats," muttered Kevin.

"Not a good start," said Ali. He blew the whistle and one of the monkeys jumped into the water, swam to the ball, and brought it back.

More alligators had gathered in the water to watch, just their heads and backs breaking the surface. Frankie began to worry what would happen if they failed. The alligators looked hungry.

Louise stepped up next. She kicked the ball low, so the wind couldn't catch it. It skimmed across the surface a couple of times, but still fell short by about twenty metres. Charlie patted her on the back. "Good try," he said.

"Anyone feeling peckish?" said Ali. "That little dog will do as an appetiser."

Max backed away. "Don't count your canines," he said. "We've one more go."

When the sodden monkey brought the ball again, he looked at

Frankie sadly. "Good luck," he said.
"We're all rooting for you."

"Yeah," squawked a parrot.
"Since he got that whistle, he's
been insufferable. He's even got the
sloths running round for him, and
the sloths hate running *anywhere*."

Frankie narrowed his eyes.
Seeing Lou's shot had given him an
idea. "Hey, Ali," he said. "Maybe you
should send all the other alligators
away so they don't see you lose
your bet."

The alligator rolled his eyes.
"Really?" he chuckled. "Maybe I
should call more, so they all see *you*
lose."

Frankie shrugged and tried not to smile. "Go on then."

Ali blew his whistle and the water swarmed with more alligators, snapping and thrashing. Soon the river was almost blocked with their bodies.

Frankie dropped the ball on the river bank. He knew he'd only get one chance – this kick needed to be accurate.

"Let's get this over with," said Ali.

Frankie kicked the ball. It shot low over the water then bounced on an alligator's head. Then it bounced again, and again, and again, ricocheting off the bridge

of reptiles. It skidded on to the far
bank and Frankie's friends cheered.
A few monkeys joined in too, but
they stopped when Ali blew his
whistle.

"So can we have the whistle
now?" said Frankie.

Ali narrowed his eyes. "No. You
cheated."

He sank beneath the water, and Frankie saw the shape of his body swim off towards an island in the middle of the river. The other alligators vanished, leaving Frankie and his companions on the bank with the monkeys, the jaguars, the parrots and the snakes.

"What now?" said Max.

Frankie clenched his fists. He *hadn't* cheated. He'd used his brain. *Well, if the alligator won't give me what he promised, I'll have to take it for myself.*

He glanced at the animals. "Do you want your lives back?" he said.

"Yes!" chorused the animals.

"Then we need your help," said Frankie.

"Anything," said a monkey.

Frankie grinned. "Time to put Plan B into action!"

The jaguars had dragged the fallen branches over in their jaws, and the monkeys had found the vines to tie them together. It hadn't taken the friends long to make a raft. Now, Frankie and his friends used their hands to paddle towards Alligator Island. It was hard to fight against the current, and they were all breathing hard.

"I hope you know what you're doing," said Kevin.

So do I, thought Frankie. *If the snakes don't do their bit, we'll be dinner.*

Ali and his friends saw them approaching, and waddled to where their island sloped into the water. "I told you," he said. "You're not having the whistle. Now go away."

Frankie stepped off his raft into the shallows, as close as he dared. "You owe me," he said.

Ali shook his head. "Last warning," he said. "My stomach's rumbling and that means you've got about ten seconds."

The other alligators all dragged their bodies to the water's edge, licking their lips.

"I'm not scared of you," said Frankie, although, beneath the water, his knees were trembling.

"You should be," said Ali. With a flick of his tail, he surged into the water with his teeth bared. The others followed. Frankie scrambled back towards the raft, and Louise and Charlie grabbed his arms and pulled him on board.

Next moment, the alligators all came to the surface. But they weren't snapping their jaws anymore. Each one had a snake coiled around their snouts, clamping their mouths closed.

The snakes had done it! Frankie's plan was working! Ali thrashed and made a lot of "Mmmm!" sounds, but a large snake gripped him tightly. A parrot swooped down from above, gripped the whistle's cord and tugged it off. The bird flew straight up, then dropped it.

Straight towards the water.

"No!" yelled Frankie. It would sink without a trace.

Charlie's gloved hand reached from the side of the raft and snatched the whistle.

"Always ready!" said Louise.

But Charlie's lunge had rocked the raft away from the island, into the current. Suddenly they were spinning away into the fastest part of the river.

Frankie struggled to hold on as spray splashed over the raft. Max lay on his belly. "I feel sea-sick!" he whined.

Everyone's faces were twisted in panic as the raft surged down the river, out of control. Frankie tried to paddle, but he had no chance. They dipped and rose on the rapids, hanging on for dear life.

"What's that?" said Kevin, pointing downriver, drenched to the skin already.

Frankie followed his gaze and swallowed hard. Up ahead, the water seemed to vanish. This could mean only one thing.

"Paddle backwards, all of you!" said Frankie. "It's a waterfall!"

They all leapt to the edges of the raft and began frantically cupping water, trying to slow themselves down. But it was hopeless. Slowly but surely the current tugged them towards the drop.

They reached the edge, and as the makeshift boat began to dip, Frankie saw a drop of hundreds of metres below where the river plunged into a foaming cascade. His stomach yo-yoed up to his throat as gravity took hold.

Frankie closed his eyes and clutched the whistle tightly. Was it all over?

PART TWO

CHAPTER 6

"You guys look soaked!" said Ricardo.

Frankie opened his eyes and found himself and his friends in a small room. The Brazilian was lying on a table on his stomach, with one leg of his tracksuit bottoms rolled up. Frankie realised it was a physio room – he remembered that Ricardo had picked up a minor strain in his semi-final match.

Max shook himself vigorously, soaking the footballer.

"You'd be wet too if you'd almost drowned in the Amazon," he said.

The magic must have saved their skins, just in time.

"We rescued this," said Frankie. He opened his fist and held the whistle by its cord. Ricardo leapt off the bench.

"Well done!" he said. "I should never have doubted you!"

"Did you doubt us?" asked Charlie, frowning.

Ricardo smiled lopsidedly. "Only a little."

"Listen," said Louise. "What's really going on here? Who actually took these things?"

"There isn't much time, but I can tell you a bit," said Ricardo. He clicked his fingers towards a TV on the wall and the screen blinked on. It showed a huge house on a hill, with sprawling lawns all around. There was an artificial pitch to one side, and a boy was doing tricks with a football, his feet a blur as he bounced it up and down, catching it behind his head and doing stepovers.

"Is that you?" asked Kevin. "I thought you were supposed to have grown up in a slum."

Ricardo shook his head. "That is Diego," he said. "He had a very different upbringing to me, as you can see. While I played barefoot, using sweatshirts for goalposts, he had everything he could ever wish for. His own pitch, the best kit, even a coach. His parents were very wealthy. Diego was always the best."

"I've never heard of him," said Frankie.

"That's because he stopped practising," said Ricardo. "He used to call me names when I stayed later than everyone else to work on my technique. He knew there was something special about my football." He pointed to the magic football in Louise's hands. "But by the time we tried out for the national under–16 side, Diego had grown lazy. I was selected ahead of him."

"Wait — you had the magic football?" said Charlie.

The Brazilian nodded. "Diego was jealous and he stole the ball from me. He became lost in the magical football world for over two years, playing games through history and all over the world!"

"Until now," said Louise.

Ricardo nodded. "He must have found a way out, and he wants his revenge against the game."

"More importantly," said Kevin. "How are England doing?"

"Let's see, shall we?" said Ricardo. He clicked his fingers again and the TV switched channel to the

82

England match. Frankie saw there were only five minutes left and it was still one–one. Not only that, but half the crowd seemed to have gone home. Two players were lying on the pitch injured, and as they watched an Argentine defender flattened the England striker right in front of goal. The ref blew his whistle and pointed to the penalty spot.

"*Yes*!" said Frankie. "We've got to win now."

The England striker picked himself up, and placed his ball on the spot.

Frankie sensed the whole room

holding its breath with him as the striker jogged forward, swung his boot . . .

. . . and kicked the ball high over the bar.

Max groaned.

"England won't get to the Final playing like that," said Louise.

"Don't you see?" said Ricardo. "Fair play has been restored, but until you find the match ball, the players have no skills. And there won't *be* a Final, unless you can find the trophy."

Frankie's boots began to tingle again. "Something's happening," he said.

He heard footsteps outside the door. "Quick, my doctor's coming back!" said Ricardo.

As the door handle turned, the room vanished.

Frankie found himself surrounded by dancing people. Drums boomed and maracas clacked and horns blasted all around him. Max scampered between his ankles to avoid getting trodden on.

"We're at a carnival!" said Louise. "We must be in Rio de Janeiro!"

The river of people was slowly making its way down the street, and it was hard for Frankie to

even stay close to his companions.
They pushed their way towards
the pavement. The road they were
on led down to the beach and
the sea, where lights sparkled on
the water. People were wearing
incredible costumes in every colour
under the sun. Huge floats rolled
down the street as well, with more
people dancing on top of them, or
throwing sparkling confetti over
the sides. Some had acrobats doing
flips, or jumping up in the splits.

Normally, Frankie would have
loved it, but today there was a more
pressing matter.

How are we ever going to find

the trophy or the ball here? There must be thousands of people!

Then he saw it. Coming towards them was a float shaped like a giant football. A juggler on stilts walked in front of it, tossing five footballs into the air. As the float moved past, Frankie saw that a section of the huge orb was cut away, and sitting inside was a skinny young man in a pristine white tracksuit. He had slicked-back dark hair and he was sipping on a drink from a coconut shell. Gold rings covered his fingers. His face was set in a scowl.

Frankie peered closer. "That's Diego!" he said.

CHAPTER 7

"He looks like the only person not enjoying the carnival," said Louise.

"Makes sense," said Charlie.

"We need to get on board."

They followed the float, which was moving at a slow walking pace, then clambered on to the back. Max was too small to climb

up, so Frankie tossed him up to
Charlie, and hopped on board
himself. No one seemed to notice
them getting on — everyone was
having too much fun. Frankie kept
his eyes peeled for traps as he
crept forwards. *It can't be this
easy . . .*

Diego had his back to them, but
Frankie spotted a football under his
left foot. It was definitely a World
Cup ball, with green, blue and
orange swirls. Perhaps the trophy
was here too and they could get
both things at the same time.

Frankie turned to his friends and
placed a finger to his lips. If they

could stay quiet, he might be able to sneak up and . . .

"Did little Ricardihno send you?" said Diego, without turning around.

Frankie stopped. "Your game has gone on long enough," he said.

Diego pressed a button in the arm of his chair and it revolved to face Frankie. He tossed his drink aside, wiping a sleeve across his mouth. "This isn't a game," he sneered. "It's a war — a war against football!"

Frankie approached slowly, keeping his eye on the ball.

"I see my old friend has got only

the best to come after me," he said
sarcastically. "A bunch of kids —
pathetic!"

Frankie sensed his friends
fanning out behind him. "Give us
the ball," said Louise.

"Come and get it," said Diego.

Max darted from behind
Frankie's legs, and tried to clamp
his teeth over the ball. Diego
pressed a button on the arm of
his throne, and a net shot from
the floor, closing over the dog.
He rolled over several times,
hopelessly tangled and barking
madly. "Silly mutt!" said Diego.
"Who's next?"

Louise ran at him, and Diego
pressed another button. Some sort
of liquid shot from the underside of
his seat, and Louise skidded. She
winced in pain and clutched her
ankle.

"Oil!" she said.

"I learned a few tricks, trapped in
that world for so long," said Diego.

Charlie, Frankie noticed, was sneaking up from the other side. Diego pressed another button and a blast of fire surged towards him. Charlie backed away, gloves in front of his face. The crowd around the float oohed and aahed. *They think it's just a trick,* thought Frankie.

Charlie took off his gloves and stamped the fire out. His face was pale with anger. "I can't believe you made me take my gloves off!" he said. "I *never* take my gloves off."

"Maybe it's time you left me alone," said Diego. "Before someone gets hurt."

Frankie didn't dare take a step

closer. Who knew what other tricks Diego had up his sleeve?

"Hey, look what I found!" called Kevin. Frankie turned and saw his brother poking his head through a hatch in the float.

"No! Get away from there!" shouted Diego.

"What is it?" called Frankie.

Suddenly the whole float rocked forward sharply, throwing Frankie off his feet. Diego tumbled from the chair, landing on his football.

"The brake lever!" said Kevin.

The float began to rumble more quickly down the street. Kevin had let off all the brakes and now the float could travel fast — too fast. People screamed as they tried to scramble out of the way. The juggler toppled from his stilts, landing on an awning above a shop. His footballs bounced off down the street among the panicking carnival-goers. The float picked up even more speed, surging down towards the beach. Someone was going to get flattened.

"Stop it!" screamed Louise.

"Okay, okay!" said Kevin, ducking down again.

With a deafening screech, the float juddered to a halt, sliding

sideways. Frankie saw the ball
roll free of Diego's grip, and drop
off the edge of the float into the
seething crowd.

"Get the ball!" he shouted to
his friends. He leapt off the float,
landing in a crouch on the ground.
He saw the ball bouncing back and
forth between hundreds of pairs
of feet. Louise climbed down after
him, limping slightly and helped by
Kevin. Charlie was untangling Max
from the net.

"Sorry," said Kevin. "I thought if I
caused a distraction . . ."

"You certainly did that!" said
Louise.

Diego jumped over their heads and ran after the ball. Frankie was hot on his heels.

"You'll never beat me!" shouted Diego over his shoulder. He dropped into a slide, tripping several people as he reached the ball. "Ha!" he cried. He picked up the ball and ran off towards the beach.

Frankie sprinted in pursuit across the sand. Diego was quick at first, but soon he was panting. *Should've practised more,* thought Frankie. Eventually, Diego stopped to face Frankie, glaring defiantly. "You'll never have the ball!" he said. He turned to the sea, and kicked the ball so far out into the water that Frankie couldn't even see it any more.

Diego gave Frankie a cruel grin, but then his face fell. "What?" he said, looking left and right.

Frankie span around and saw that his friends had arrived, and they all had a different ball at their feet. *Of course!* thought Frankie. *The juggler dropped them all!*

"So which one is the real one?" said Kevin. "They all look the same to me."

"This one!" said Ricardo. He strode down the beach, holding a ball. "I hope you don't mind. I managed to slip away from my hotel."

"You!" hissed Diego.

"Hello, old friend," said Ricardo.

Diego kicked the sand. "We're not friends. You *stole* my place on the team. You *left* me in that fantasy world."

"You know that isn't true," said Ricardo. He faced Frankie and his friends. "Thank you, by the way — England just won with an amazing header in extra time. They're through to the Final."

"Hurray!" said Louise. She threw her arms around Charlie, who blushed.

"You took *everything* from me," said Diego, "but you won't have . . . THIS!"

With a flash of light, the golden trophy appeared in his hand.

CHAPTER 8

Frankie stared. "Is that the real World Cup?"

"It's *my* real World Cup," said Diego.

"It's for real *winners*, not thieves," said Ricardo.

Diego's face darkened. "What have you ever won?" he said. "It's time to see who's really the best. I'll give you the trophy if you and your team can beat me and mine. Can't say fairer than that."

Ricardo looked at Frankie and his friends, biting his lip. "I don't know . . ."

"We'll do it," said Frankie. "But where are *your* team?"

Diego grinned. "They're coming," he said. He held the World Cup over his head and gold rays of light shot from the top. As they hit the sand, shapes began to appear – the outlines of figures. Frankie glanced about to see if anyone was watching, but the beach was deserted apart from them. As the golden light faded away, five players stood beside Diego.

"Meet my team," he said. He pointed first to an Asian boy – "This is Tanaki." Next came a girl with long blonde hair. "And Hanna, from Germany." Then two stocky identical dark–skinned boys stepped up, folding their arms. "Meet Xander and Benji," said Diego. Last of all came a girl at least six feet tall. "And my goalkeeper, from the USA, Mindy."

None of the opposing players said a word – and from the blank look in their eyes Frankie guessed something weird was going on. It was like they were robots.

"Where did you find this team of yours?" asked Louise.

Diego shrugged. "These are all the previous owners of the magic football," he said. "The best of their generations. You want to earn the trophy, these are the players you have to beat."

"Now wait a minute, Diego . . ." said Ricardo.

"The game will be sudden death," said Diego, as his players spread out behind him. Frankie realised it was six-a-side, which suited him fine. *We have Ricardo, after all!* Goal posts had magically sprouted from the sand at opposite ends of the beach, and Mindy took her place between one set. Charlie ran to the other, kicking up sand as he went. Frankie realised he wasn't wearing his gloves.

Frankie pointed to both wings, and Louise and Max took up positions. Kevin stood in front of Charlie's goal, ready to defend.

"Come on!" said Frankie to Ricardo. "We need you up front."

Ricardo shook his head. "I can't play."

"*What?*" said all of Frankie's team at the same time.

"I just . . . don't feel like it," said Ricardo. "Plus, what if I get injured?"

Frankie couldn't believe what he was hearing.

"You brought us here," said Kevin. "What's the matter with you? The World Cup is at stake!"

Diego chuckled. "Don't you get it?" he said. "His spirit has gone. He doesn't care anymore. Now, ready to start?"

"But we've only got five players," said Louise.

"I know," said Diego, with a sly grin. "I'll let you kick off, since you have the ball."

Frankie looked down at his feet, where the magic football rested on the sand. He had one chance to save the World Cup.

And he wasn't going to blow it.

He passed the ball sideways to Louise, but it skidded then died on the loose sand. Hanna pounced on it quickly, chipped the ball over Louise's tackle, then lofted the ball towards Tanaki. It was way too high for Max, and Tanaki met it with his head, leaping above Kevin, and powering a shot towards Charlie's goal. Frankie watched with his heart in his mouth as Charlie dived.

Slap!

He saved it with his palm. Just. Charlie rubbed his hand. "Ouch!"

"Nice work!" Frankie shouted, as he rushed back to the goal, but he thought, *That was too close! We almost lost in the first few seconds.*

Louise came over to him and Max joined the huddle too while Kevin trudged over, looking glum. "We can't play along the ground like we do at home," she said. "We need to adapt."

"But how?" said Frankie. "We don't stand a chance."

Louise gripped his arm. "You

mustn't think like that, Frankie," she said. "You can't lose your spirit too."

"But they've got one more player than us," said Frankie. "And you heard what Diego said. These guys are the best."

No," said Max, by his feet. "Remember all the times we've pulled through."

"That's right," said Charlie. "We need you to be our captain and lead from the front."

Frankie smiled at his friends. "Okay," he said, feeling a flicker of hope. "Let's try and keep the ball in the air."

Charlie tossed it out, and Max

headed it on to Louise. She let the ball bounce.

"To me, Lou," Frankie shouted.

She dinked the ball neatly over both the twins, Xander and Benji. Frankie controlled it on his chest, then his knee. It was going perfectly. He saw Tanaki heading his way, and adjusted his body for the shot on goal.

Thump! Suddenly his feet were taken from beneath him, and Frankie hit the sand hard, the wind knocked from his lungs. He lay on his side, struggling to breathe, as Diego took the ball and darted upfield. He skipped

around first Lou, then Max, then
Kevin, leaving them all trailing.
He was one-on-one with Charlie.
Charlie rushed out, spreading his
arms, but Diego just rolled the ball
between his legs. It slotted into
the open goal.

Diego slid on to the sand, arms in
the air. "I won! I won!" he cried.

"No, you didn't," said Hanna.

Frankie frowned as he picked
himself up.

"Yes, I did," said Diego. "Look,
the ball is in the goal."

"You fouled the opposition," said
Tanaki.

Diego grabbed the ball. "I

didn't summon you here for your opinions," he said.

Mindy stepped out of goal. "Well, we're not cheats," she said. "It's a free kick to them."

Diego faced his team, and Frankie. "Fine," he said. "Let's play your way." He kicked the ball angrily back to Frankie, who set it down where the foul had happened.

"Let me take it," said Kevin.

"Frankie should take it," said Louise. "He's the captain."

Kevin stood over the ball. "Frankie's lost it," he said harshly. "You heard him. He doesn't think we can win."

Diego walked over. "I don't care who takes it," he said. "Just get on with it."

Louise was muttering something to Kevin under her breath. To Frankie's surprise, she looked sideways at him and nodded. "You're right, Kev," she said. "You should take it."

Max lay on the sand, hiding his face in his paws. Charlie's shoulders sagged.

Frankie's heart sank like a stone.

Even Louise doesn't believe in me anymore. None of my team do.

CHAPTER 9

Frankie stepped away from the ball.
It was all up to his brother now.
The other team had formed a wall
in front of the goal and Mindy was
jumping up and down on the goal
line. There was no way Kevin could
score.

"Hey, Frankenstein," said Kevin.

"Remember in the garden, before the TV broke, when we were practising and you missed the kick?"

Frankie nodded. *Of course I missed*, he thought sadly. *I should never even have tried.*

"I distracted you on purpose," said Kevin. "I . . . I knew you could do it, and I was just jealous. Because . . ." he took a deep breath. "Because you're better than me. You always have been."

Frankie could hardly believe what he was hearing. *Is my brother actually being nice to me?*

"Yeah," said Louise, with a wink.

"We *all* know you can do that kick, Frankie."

Max ran up to Frankie's leg. "Show 'em how it's done, boss," he whispered.

Frankie understood what he had to do. It was a risky plan, but it might be their only chance. He looked at Ricardo, who was standing at the water's edge. He'd put all his faith in Frankie's team. They couldn't let him down.

"Enough yapping!" said Diego.

Frankie began to walk back to his own goal, pretending to be defeated, but he watched out of the corner of his eye. As Kevin started his run-up, Frankie turned and ran at the goal. Instead of shooting, Kevin clipped the ball sideways.

"Huh?" said Diego.

Frankie watched the ball come over his shoulder, looping as if in slow motion. He flung himself into the air, jerking up his hips and bringing round his leg. He was upside-down as his foot met the ball.

Whack!

As he landed in the sand, he squirmed around to see. Mindy was sprawled in front of her goal. Her wall of defenders was staring

backwards. Frankie couldn't see the
ball. Had he scored?

"Supergooaaaaallll!" yelled
Louise.

"You did it, bro!" said Kevin,
leaping on top of him.

"Go Frankie!" screamed Charlie,
throwing himself on to the pile as
well.

Through the gap in their limbs, Frankie saw Max spinning in happy circles on the sand.

As his friends rolled off him, Frankie found himself staring at a pair of feet. Ricardo leant down beside him and held out a hand. "I recognise that kick!" he said.

Frankie blushed. "It was a 'Ricardo'," he said.

"It was better than mine," said the Brazilian. "Let's call it a 'Frankie' from now on."

Frankie took his hand and clambered to his feet. A flash of panic shot across his chest. "Where's Diego?" he said, staring down the deserted beach. "Where's his team?"

"I don't think he wanted to stick around," said Ricardo. "He always was a sore loser."

"But what about the World Cup trophy?" said Louise. "He's run off with it."

Frankie ran his hands through his hair. *After all that . . . we still haven't won the trophy . . .*

"No, he hasn't," said Charlie. "Look!"

A few metres away, Max was scrabbling at the beach with his paws, kicking up sand. Frankie saw the glint of gold metal. "It's the trophy!" he said.

Max turned round. "You should be the first to hold it, Frankie," he said.

Frankie walked over slowly with his friends. The World Cup seemed to glow, even though it was half-covered in sand. Frankie crouched down and lifted the trophy, dusting it off. He had dreamed of holding it ever since he'd first played football as a little boy. *Can this really be happening?*

"Congratulations, Team Frankie," said Ricardo. "I couldn't have picked a more worthy side. Thanks to you, the World Cup is safe."

Frankie felt a strange shiver along his arm.

"To Team Frankie!" said Louise.

"To Team Frankie," cried his friends.

Silver lights cascaded around them like the stars were falling from the sky. Frankie hoisted the trophy into the air.

"To Team . . ."

"Frankie?" said his mother's voice. "We're home!"

Frankie was standing in his living room, with his friends at his side. His hand was empty. Any feeling of triumph sapped away. The TV was still propped up at an angle, the screen shattered. Kevin looked terrified. "Frankie?" called his mother again. "Kevin?"

Frankie ran to the door to intercept his parents, followed by the others.

In the hallway, his dad was taking off his coat. "What a bizarre game of football!" he said. "For a few minutes it was like watching kids play!"

"Dad, there's been an accident," Frankie began.

"Can't complain, I suppose," continued his father. "No one would have picked England for the Final, would they?"

Frankie's mother had frozen, staring into the lounge.

"I can explain," said Frankie.

His dad had seen the wrecked TV too now. He turned to face Frankie. "Well, you'd better start right now," he said.

Frankie took a deep breath, and realised he couldn't think of a single thing to say.

Three days later, Frankie and Kevin were sitting in their bedroom,

feeling very sorry for themselves.
Frankie was fiddling with the dial
on his dad's old radio.

"I can't find it!" he said. "What's
the station?"

Max whined, not for the first
time that evening.

"This is *so* unfair," said Kevin. " I
can't believe we're not allowed to
watch the World Cup Final."

Frankie heard a crackle, then the
announcer's voice. *"And welcome
to Rio, for a night that hosts one o
the most eagerly anticipated games
for a generation. The Three Lions
take on the might of Brazil."*

The voice drifted into static again

"I mean, you wait nearly fifty years for England to make the Final, and we're stuck up here without a TV to watch it on," grumbled Kevin.

Frankie could hardly blame his parents for grounding them. The TV was an expensive one, and now his dad had to go to his mother-in-law's to watch the football, and he didn't like that at all! Charlie had said he'd record the game anyway, so they could watch it properly another time. They had to be content with the radio.

"*. . . and there it is,*" said the announcer. "*The trophy both teams*

are playing for. The most famous
reward in the world of sport . . ."

Frankie smiled to himself,
imagining the World Cup being
shown on screen. To think,
just three days ago he'd won it
himself!

"I doubt we'll ever get chance
again," Kevin said. "Or if we do,
we'll be so ancient we can't play
anymore . . ."

"*What are you guys doing in your
bedroom?"* said the radio.

Max's ears pricked up and
Frankie jolted upright.

"Was that Ricardo's voice?" said
Frankie's brother.

"*It should be,*" said the Brazilian. "*Because it is me.*"

Frankie turned the radio volume up. "Hello?" he said. "Where are you?"

"*I'm in the tunnel,*" said Ricardo. "*About to go on to the pitch for the World Cup Final. I just remembered I forgot to give you something.*"

"What?" said Frankie, feeling a bit foolish talking to a radio.

"*Your VIP tickets,*" said the voice.

Frankie's bedroom vanished, and his stomach flipped as he found himself high in the packed stands overlooking a bright green pitch. The noise around him was deafening — thousands of fans chanting and singing and blowing horns. Kevin was sitting on one side, Louise and Charlie on the other. "We're really here, aren't we?" said Louise. "At the World Cup Final."

"Will someone lift me up so I can actually see?" said a voice.

Frankie looked down and saw a furry face peering out beneath his seat. He placed Max on his lap. "There you go, boy."

"Er . . . how did that happen?" asked Charlie. Frankie grinned to see he was wearing a new pair of gloves.

The teams were coming out on to the pitch, England in their red away strip, Brazil in yellow and blue. A player halfway along the Brazilian line turned to them and waved. It was their friend, Ricardo.

"We were sent a special invite," said Frankie, waving back. "One last bit of magic."

The best magic they'd seen so far!

ACKNOWLEDGEMENTS

Many thanks to everyone at
Little, Brown Book Group; Neil
Blair, Zoe King, Daniel Teweles
and all at The Blair Partnership;
Luella Wright for bringing my
characters to life; special thanks
to Michael Ford for all his wisdom
and patience; and to Steve

Kutner for being a great friend and for all his help and guidance, not just with the book but with everything.

FRANKIE'S MAGIC FOOTBALL

COULD YOU BE A WINNER, LIKE FRANKIE?

Take a look at the pictures in this book. Somewhere, we have hidden a miniature Brazilian flag, just like this one:

Can you find it?

For the chance to win an exclusive

Frankie's Magic Football goodie bag, write down the page number this secret image appears on then visit www.lbkids.co.uk/frankiecomp and ask a grown up to help you fill in the form.

Once you've completed your entry, you will be able to download a template to colour in your own Brazil flag.

This competition is open to all readers. Closing date is 31st July 2014. For full terms and conditions, see the website.

Frankie wishes you all good luck. Remember, everyone has talent!